THE
ACCUSER

Anne Schraff

◼️QREADS

SADDLEBACK
EDUCATIONAL PUBLISHING
www.sdlback.com

ISBN-13: 978-1-61651-188-3
ISBN-10: 1-61651-188-5
eBook: 978-1-60291-910-5

Printed in the U.S.A.

21 20 19 18 17   5 6 7 8 9

■ ■ ■

Donyell Mason had always looked up to his big brother, Ricky. Not that Ricky was some kind of angel. When things didn't go his way, the tough 20-year-old could be mean. But to Donyell, two years younger, Ricky was pretty much a personal hero. Nobody pushed Donyell around if Ricky had anything to say about it. And he always did.

Nobody pushed Ricky around, either—at least not until big Beau Patterson came along. Ricky was bigger than most guys, but Beau outweighed him by 50 pounds or more. And Beau was a dirty fighter.

Last week Ricky said that Beau had been getting in his face and hassling him. Donyell was startled to hear that. He had never seen such a look of pure hatred on his brother's face.

■ ■ ■

Now it was late on a Monday night, and Ricky wasn't home yet. Ricky was a good mechanic. He worked long hours at the A-1 Garage, but it was unusual when he wasn't in by 11:00.

Donyell finally went to bed in the room he shared with his brother, but he couldn't get to sleep. Maybe Beau had waylaid his brother and tried to rob him. Maybe Ricky was lying hurt in some alley right now.

Suddenly the door opened and Donyell stiffened. It always irked Ricky when Donyell worried about him, so Donyell pretended to be asleep. But he listened for the familiar sounds Ricky made when he came home. He needed assurance that everything was all right.

When it was late like this, Ricky always took a quick shower and came right to bed.

But tonight was different. Ricky showered for a long time. Then Donyell heard a garbage bag rustling. Finally, Ricky came into the bedroom. Donyell peered at his brother in the darkness and almost cried out.

Ricky's face was badly bruised and bloodied. He looked like he'd been in a terrible fight! Stifling the gasp on his lips, Donyell watched Ricky climb stiffly into bed. The poor guy was hurting all over. He groaned, as if any movement brought pain. After a while, he finally seemed to fall asleep.

When Donyell was sure his brother was asleep, he quietly got out of bed. He went to the bathroom and found Ricky's wet T-shirt hanging over the tub. Then Donyell followed a trail of blood drops to the trash container in the kitchen. He opened the garbage bag wadded up on top and saw that Ricky's jeans and shoes were bloody.

"Oh, man, something *bad* happened," Donyell whispered to himself.

Then the kitchen door slammed open and

Ricky was glaring at his kid brother. "What're you doing, you little creep? Spying on me?"

"No," Donyell sputtered. "I was just worried when you came home so late. Then I heard funny sounds and—uh— things just didn't seem right."

"Go on back to bed, Don. Forget all this—you hear what I'm saying? You didn't see anything and you didn't hear anything. Understand?" Ricky growled. "It was an accident. I stumbled into an old Chevy I was fixing and got messed up. I cut myself, okay?"

"Sure, okay," Donyell mumbled.

But of course it wasn't okay at all. It wasn't anything like okay.

■ ■ ■

Donyell was taking a graphic arts class at the local community college. He had to get up early even though he hadn't had much sleep. As usual, he gulped his breakfast and ran out to catch the early bus to school. Another guy from the neighborhood was taking classes at City College, too. Donyell and Jerry Kelton had been friends since grade school. They usually sat together on the bus. Donyell was a good-looking guy and a pretty fair athlete. Jerry was a short, skinny kid with thick glasses and a bad case of acne.

"What's going down, buddy?" Jerry called out when Donyell arrived at the bus stop. Jerry looked a little more nervous than usual. He was fidgeting with his baseball cap, turning it around every which way before he settled it on his head with the bill down the back of his neck. He was always trying to look tough—but he was like a fuzzy little kitten trying to look like a wildcat.

"Nothing much," Donyell said. But he needed information. He wanted to talk to somebody, to fish for news of a possible fight last night. "I heard there was some trouble on the street last night. You hear anything like that, Jerry?"

"Huh? Like gangbangers, you mean?" Jerry asked.

"I don't know. I just heard something about a fight," Donyell said. He didn't want to say too much. Maybe Ricky and a pal were just playing around and it got out of hand. A good fistfight can bloody noses pretty fast.

Jerry sat down on the bench beside Donyell. "Yeah, I heard something was going on, all right. It was probably some of those guys who only come out when the sun don't shine. They're like rats—you hear what I'm saying? Those guys are bad news."

"What guys are you talking about?" Donyell asked nervously.

Jerry turned his head sharply. "I don't know. How should I know? I don't mess with anybody. I learned that lesson a long time ago."

■ ■ ■

Donyell knew what his friend was saying. Jerry had always been a scared, little guy. In middle school he often went hungry because it was so easy for bigger, meaner kids to get his lunch money. All it took was a threat to flatten his nose; Jerry always paid. Donyell understood how that went. When he

8

was in middle school the same thing could easily have happened to him. But Ricky alway stood up for him. Jerry never had a protector.

"I wonder what really happened last night," Donyell went on as they boarded the bus.

"How should I know?" Jerry said again, a flash of anger in his eyes. "What do you think I am—a cop?"

At Fourth and Aspen, Donyell noticed that the street was roped off with yellow crime scene tape. A few seats back on the bus, a girl said to her friend, "Look—that's where it happened. Right there on the corner is where Beau Patterson died last night."

Donyell couldn't breathe. He felt like somebody had hit him in the stomach with a two-by-four.

■ ■ ■

Donyell and Jerry got off at the next stop. "Jerry, did you hear that girl talking?" Donyell blurted out. "She said

Beau Patterson is *dead*!"

"You want me to cry or something?" Jerry shot back. "That dude was no friend of mine. He bullied everybody. I'm *glad* he won't be around anymore."

"You knew about it already, didn't you?" Donyell asked in surprise.

"Yeah. There was something on the radio this morning," Jerry said.

"How come you didn't tell me? How come you acted so stupid when I asked if you knew anything about a fight last night?" Donyell demanded.

"Man," Jerry said, "I didn't know about a *fight*. I just heard they found a dead guy on Aspen. Then the man next door told me it was Beau Patterson. Maybe he got hit by a garbage truck. How should I know?"

Donyell's mind was in turmoil as he walked alone to his art class. He didn't think Beau was hit by any garbage truck. The odds were that he was killed in a fight. And from the looks of Ricky last night, *he'd* been in a fight, too. Maybe both of them had been in the same fight.

Class was already in session when Donyell took his seat. He tried to concentrate on the computer. The whole class was working on a series of color graphics for a model advertising campaign. Eventually, Donyell hoped to work for a company that made print and television commercials. But as hard as he tried to concentrate, Ricky's battered face kept coming back to him. And he couldn't stop thinking about the bloody shoes and pants in the garbage bag.

■ ■ ■

When Donyell got home from school, the apartment was empty. Ricky was probably at work. He made pretty good money at the garage. He could do mechanical work as skillfully as his boss, who was twice his age. The boss, Mr. Kenyon, had told Ricky that he was the best young mechanic that had ever worked for him. He had a great future.

Two years earlier, the boys' mother had

died. She was the only parent either of them had ever known. Ricky was just 18 then, but he took over, making sure that Donyell had a stable home life. Donyell owed *everything* to his brother. He loved him a lot—even when he was bossy or mean. Donyell didn't need to be told to keep his mouth shut about last night. He would never rat his brother out—no matter what it cost him.

But that didn't keep his stomach from churning with worry. He looked in the kitchen and saw that the garbage bag with the bloody jeans and shoes was gone. The drops of blood in the hallway were gone, too. There was not a thing in the apartment to connect Ricky to whatever had happened at Fourth and Aspen last night.

What if there had been witnesses? Maybe somebody had seen Ricky there! If the police showed up and started asking questions, Ricky's bruised face would make them very suspicious. Nobody got messed up like that just wrestling with a transmission. If Beau Patterson had been beaten to death,

Donyell's brother would be a prime suspect. Everybody on the street knew there was bad blood between Ricky Mason and Beau Patterson.

Donyell flipped on the television. First there was a lot of news about the heat wave and wildfires burning in the mountains. Then the anchorwoman said, *"Police are investigating the death of twenty-year-old Beau Patterson. The young man's body was discovered at the corner of Fourth and Aspen last night. Police are not ruling out gang connections in the homicide. Any witnesses are asked to come forward to help in the investigation. A clerk in a nearby convenience store has already reported seeing two young men having a violent argument in the vicinity. The time of the incident is estimated to have been about 10:30 P.M."*

Oh, no! Donyell's blood ran cold. Ricky had come home around 11:00. It was entirely possible he and Patterson had been fighting at 10:30.

Anything could have happened. Ricky

could have stopped off for pizza, and Patterson might have jumped him. Or maybe they had started talking trash to each other and things got out of hand. The TV news report didn't say what Patterson's injuries were. For fear of damaging trial evidence, the police didn't release that kind of information.

Deep in the pit of his stomach, Donyell somehow felt sure Ricky had been there when Patterson died. Ricky was all the family Donyell had. It made him sick to think that his big brother might soon be facing a murder rap.

■ ■ ■

Then the phone rang, and Donyell snatched it up.

"Don?" It was Ricky's voice on the other end of the line.

"Yeah, Ricky. Hey, I just found out that Beau Patterson got himself killed last night. It's all over the TV and—" Donyell began, but Ricky cut him off.

"Look, kid, I haven't got no time to talk.

I'm taking a couple days off from the garage. I'm with some friends, okay?" Ricky sounded really nervous. His words came out in rapid, short bursts like machine gun fire.

"Ricky, are you in trouble?" Donyell asked. He realized immediately what a stupid question that was. *Of course* he was in trouble. He must have called his boss with some excuse. He had to lay low. It would raise eyebrows for sure if he showed up at the garage with a face that looked like raw hamburger.

"I just need to be away for a couple days, that's all. Keep cool, Donyell. And remember—you never saw me come home so late last night, right? If the police come snooping around, I was home at nine-thirty. You got that? I was really tired from working at the garage, and I hit the mattress at ten," Ricky said.

"Ricky!" Donyell yelled desperately. "What's going down? I gotta know what's happening, man."

But Ricky had already hung up. Donyell stared at the dead phone in his hand. If

Ricky had killed Beau Patterson in a fight, he seemed to be leaving his 18-year-old brother to cover for him and face the consequences alone.

■ ■ ■

A hot surge of resentment boiled up in Donyell's stomach. He couldn't lie Ricky's way out of this one—not when there was a dead body. Sure, Patterson was a creep—but he was a human being. You couldn't murder somebody just because he was a creep.

Donyell had planned to go to the movies that night with his girlfriend, Vicki. He was in no mood to watch a funny movie with anybody. But he needed to get out of the apartment, so he picked her up at 7:30.

As they waited for the movie to start, Vicki seemed eager to talk. "Donyell, the word on the street is that your brother and Beau Patterson were together last night," she said.

"Impossible," Donyell said. "Ricky came home early. He ate a quick dinner and was snoring away by ten o'clock." The lie flowed easily off his lips.

"Everybody's saying—" Vicki began. "Do you believe everything you hear? Everybody is *crazy,* girl!" Donyell snapped.

Vicki backed off. "Everybody hated Beau. He was a bad guy. He even beat up on his girlfriend, Connie Jarvis. A couple of times he beat her bad. Maybe she just got so tired of him hitting on her that she busted him over the head with a baseball bat. I know a guy who saw Beau's body. The guy said his head was busted in good—"

Ice water flowed through Donyell's veins. He didn't think he could take much more.

■ ■ ■

Later that night, after Donyell took Vicki home, he walked down to the corner of Fourth and Aspen. It wasn't a great neighborhood. Nothing was there but 99¢ stores, secondhand shops, liquor stores, and bars.

Donyell decided to hang around a while. He hoped to hear something that would clear

Ricky. Before long he spotted two guys who used to be buds with Beau. They glared at Donyell like they knew something. Donyell quickly joined a group of guys he knew.

A casual friend named Jimmy greeted him. "Hey, man, the cops are grilling little Connie Jarvis about knocking off Patterson—did you hear?"

Donyell stiffened. He'd gone to high school with Connie. She was a nice kid—but she wasn't the sharpest fork in the drawer. When she'd started hanging with Beau, it had taken her a while to see how mean he was. But she finally had the sense to drop him. Maybe that was what the fatal fight was about! But it was hard for Donyell to imagine a nice girl like Connie harming anybody.

Anyway, how did that explain Ricky's chewed-up face and his strange behavior last night?

"The cops are on the wrong track. I don't think Connie did it," Donyell said. "I don't know," Jimmy said. "She's a pretty strong girl. She plays killer volleyball. That girl takes no prisoners."

"Connie's a sweet kid," Donyell said.

"Well, have *you* got any idea who killed Patterson?" Jimmy asked.

"No. I've got no idea," Donyell said. "Gotta go." He went into the convenience store that was run by a couple from Iraq. Donyell liked them because they were fair and friendly. They didn't hassle kids like a lot of merchants did.

"Lot of excitement around here last night, huh?" Donyell asked Hamid.

"Yeah, you bet. I'm glad I was here instead of my wife. She would've got plenty scared," Hamid said.

"You see anything?" Donyell asked.

"Yeah, I saw these two guys fighting. I couldn't see their faces or anything— but the big guy was pushing the shorter guy around. Then another big guy showed up. I figured something bad was going to happen, so I locked up early. I don't want any trouble," Hamid said.

Donyell nodded. He picked up a package of chocolate chip cookies and took them to the counter. Hamid smiled and said, "Your big brother and his girlfriend were in here yesterday around noon. They bought sandwiches. He's got a real pretty girlfriend."

Donyell was shocked. Ricky never said anything about a girlfriend. Then Hamid said, "Your brother's girlfriend must be an athlete, huh? I saw her name on her jacket—*Jarvis.*"

■ ■ ■

Donyell stumbled over his own feet as he walked out the door. Ricky was dating Connie Jarvis? How stupid was that? It was like playing with matches over a barrel of gasoline.

But it was *like* Ricky to do something like that! He'd always admired the pretty, dark-eyed girl who was the heaviest hitter on the championship Lincoln Lynx volleyball team. Then Donyell remembered Ricky saying that Beau didn't deserve such a great girl. If he mistreated her one more time, Ricky had said, ol' Beau would be sorry.

Maybe Beau hurt Connie again—and Ricky had gone after him. But why didn't Ricky own up to it? If he was protecting Connie, he could plead self-defense. Why didn't he come forward and explain that the killing had been an accident?

■ ■ ■

Donyell went to the apartment complex where Connie Jarvis lived with her aunt. When she answered the bell, the aunt seemed annoyed that her niece had a caller so late at night.

"Look at the time! Don't you have any sense at all?" she asked crossly.

"Auntie, is that Donyell Mason?" Connie called from a back room. "It's okay. I'll go talk to him. Don't worry— I'll be quick." Connie stepped outside into the cool night air.

"Hi, Donyell," she said. "What's up?"

"I heard the police were talking to you about Beau Patterson getting killed,"

Donyell said.

"Yeah, they talked to everybody who knew Beau. I couldn't help them much. We broke up about a month ago. I got real tired of his rough stuff," Connie said.

"I didn't know you and my brother were dating, Connie," Donyell said. "Were you guys together last night?" Connie blinked. "What're you getting at, Donyell? You mad at me, or what? There's nothing wrong with Ricky and me dating. I made a big mistake hanging with Beau. So now I'm smart enough to get a good guy. What's wrong with that?" she asked defensively.

"You didn't answer me, Connie. Were you hanging with Ricky last night?" Donyell demanded in a sharper voice.

Now Connie was angry. *"No!* But what if I was?" she cried out. "It's none of your business."

"Maybe somebody saw you and Ricky near where Beau Patterson was killed. Maybe dating you has gotten my brother into bad trouble, girl," Donyell said.

■ ■ ■

Boy, are you weird!" Connie snapped. "I didn't even *see* Ricky last night. Cross my heart, Donyell. I don't know what you're talking about!"

"Connie," the aunt called from inside the house. "Tell that boy to get himself home now—you hear me?"

"I'm coming, Auntie," Connie called. Then she turned to Donyell and said in a hard voice, "You think Ricky and I killed Beau? Is that what you think happened? Well, *I wasn't there.* I don't know what your brother did last night, but it had nothing to do with me, okay? Ricky couldn't stand Beau—even before we started hanging together!" Then Connie darted inside, slamming the door behind her.

Donyell stood there, staring at the closed door. What if Ricky had killed Beau to protect this girl? He'd be crazy to cover for her—but that was the kind of guy Ricky was. He'd take the fall rather than let a girl he loved get hurt.

Ricky had been all wrong about her. Donyell could tell that she didn't care if Ricky was in trouble because of her. She wasn't sweet. She was cold and selfish.

Hamid had seen a big person and a smaller one that night. Donyell figured it must have been Connie and Beau. Then Ricky came along, and the deadly fight started. Donyell wondered how he could convince Connie to tell the truth.

That night Donyell had a nightmare. In his dream, he was at state prison visiting Ricky—who'd been convicted of murder. Ricky had grown very bitter and sad. He didn't seem to care about anything anymore—not even Donyell. "Man," Donyell wept, "you're all the family I got, Ricky!"

"You got no family then, boy," Ricky had growled. "By the time I get out of here I won't even remember you."

With those words echoing in his ears, Donyell woke up in a cold sweat.

■ ■ ■

Early the next morning, the police came to Donyell's door. They wanted to talk to Ricky.

"He went off to the mountains for the weekend," Donyell said. "I'm not sure just when he's getting back."

When the police left, Donyell figured they'd be keeping their eyes on the apartment. They'd be ready to grab Ricky the minute he showed up.

An hour later, the phone rang. Donyell thought it would be Ricky, asking if the cops were around. But it was Jerry Kelton. "Hey, buddy—want to hang out this afternoon?" Jerry asked.

"Nah. I gotta stay home," Donyell said. "I'm—uh—expecting a phone call."

"How about me coming over there then?" Jerry asked. A shy loner, Jerry had no real friend besides Donyell.

"Okay," Donyell said. He was feeling pretty lousy anyway. May as well let him come.

Maybe it would help to have Jerry hanging out with him.

Jerry came right over. "Where's Ricky?" he asked when he sat down on the couch.

"He went off with some other guys—uh—on a fishing trip," Donyell said.

"Oh, yeah?" Jerry said. He had a strange look on his face, like he knew more than he was willing to say. Donyell wondered what was going on. Maybe people were already talking. Maybe, Donyell thought sadly, it was already on the street that the cops wanted Ricky for killing Beau Patterson.

■ ■ ■

Tell me something, Jerry. Did you know Ricky and Connie Jarvis were hanging out together?" Donyell asked.

"No, I didn't. But if they were, that wasn't too smart, was it? You know—him messing with Beau's ex-girlfriend," Jerry said. "Hey, I bet that's why . . ."His voice trailed off.

"Go on. What were you going to say, Jerry?" Donyell pressed him.

Jerry frowned and started to play with his baseball cap. "Nothing. Just that Beau hated Ricky so much. But Beau was *full* of hate. That guy was bad to the bone, man—evil inside and out. Whoever killed him did the world a big favor."

"Yeah? Well, who do *you* think killed him?" Donyell asked. For the first time it occurred to Donyell that Jerry might have been hanging out there that night. Maybe he had seen what went down.

Jerry shrugged. "I don't know," he said in the weak, nasal voice that was the butt of so many of Beau's cruel jokes.

"You *sure* you don't know?" Donyell demanded.

Jerry's eyes grew big. "What're you saying, Don? Do *you* know who did it?"

Donyell was determined not to blurt out his fears. But he was in such turmoil and pain that he couldn't help it. "I'm afraid that Ricky did it to protect Connie Jarvis," Donyell said.

"No, no, not Ricky!" Jerry cried out.

"Think about it. Ricky was dating Connie.

I'm guessing that Beau came along and tried to hurt her. Then Ricky started defending her, and somehow Beau got killed. But Connie won't own up to it. She could save my brother if she told the truth, but she's too selfish."

"No," Jerry said, *"no—"*

"I love my brother so much, Jerry! And now he might be going down for murder, don't you see?" Donyell groaned.

Jerry's face was a mask of misery as Donyell went on telling his thoughts.

"Ricky works hard, and he's a *good* mechanic. He would've had his own shop in no time. He wouldn't be making chump change like most of the guys around here. Man, my brother deserved that. After Mom died, he was mother and father to me. I'm telling you, Jerry, it's just not right. *It's not fair.*"

Jerry's face grew very pale. Then he spoke out in a small voice. "Maybe I should tell you what Beau Patterson did to me."

■ ■ ■

*W*hat?" Donyell cried out."What did you say?"

Jerry seemed to be in some kind of a trance. "You know how hot it was on Sunday? Well, Beau and some of his buddies caught me alone on the street. They grabbed me—and just for fun, they locked me in the truck of Beau's car. They turned up the stereo real loud so nobody could hear me screaming. Then they went into the pool hall for a couple of hours. I heard Beau say he wanted to find out how long it took to bake a shrimp. When they finally let me out, Beau kicked me until my kidneys were screaming," Jerry said.

Donyell just stared at his friend.

"Monday night, Beau and his friends came at me again. They chased me to Fourth and Aspen. Beau said he was going to push his fist down my throat. I was scared to death. Then the other guys took off. So it was just Beau and me—until Ricky came along.

"Ricky helped me fight Beau off. But Beau had an axe handle. He knocked Ricky down with it and was about to brain him. But then he stumbled—and somehow I got the axe handle away from him. Anyway, I hit him again and again. . . ." Jerry had begun to weep.

"Ricky told me to go home. He promised not to rat me out," Jerry went on. "I was too scared to tell the cops that I killed the guy. But I can't stand this anymore. If you go to the police with me, Donyell, I'll tell them *everything*! I'm real sick of being scared."

Donyell gave Jerry a hug. "Sure I will. Everything will be okay, man," he said. "They won't come down hard on you when you explain everything that happened." A great tide of relief swept through Donyell's mind and heart. It felt like a cleansing rain after a long drought. Now he had a future again. And the brother he loved would be part of it.

After-Reading Wrap-Up

1. The title of the story refers to Donyell. Why does the author suggest that Donyell is the accuser?

2. Reading *The Accuser,* you get a feel for Donyell's neighborhood. What kinds of homes would you not see in this neighborhood? What kinds of stores would you not see here?

3. Why does Donyell think Ricky was wrong about Connie?

4. Ricky seldom appears in the story. When he does appear, he speaks harshly to Donyell. Why should we care if he's accused of murder?

5. Why is Jerry's physical appearance important in this story?

6. What made the plot of *The Accuser* interesting to you?